Dad

Mum

Lu

m

Lucy

Will

Dad

Mum

Lu

m

Lucy

Will

The Quigleys
Not For Sale

Also available by Simon Mason:

The Quigleys
The Quigleys At Large

The Quigleys
Not For Sale

Simon Mason

Illustrated by Helen Stephens

David Fickling Books
OXFORD · NEW YORK

THE QUIGLEYS NOT FOR SALE
A DAVID FICKLING BOOK : 0 385 607547

Published in Great Britain by David Fickling Books,
an imprint of Random House Children's Books

PRINTING HISTORY
This edition published 2004

1 3 5 7 9 10 8 6 4 2

Text copyright © 2004 by Simon Mason
Illustrations copyright © 2004 by Helen Stephens

The right of Simon Mason to be identified as the author of this work has been asserted
in accordance with the Copyright, Designs and Patents Act 1988

Set in 16/20pt Bembo Schoolbook by
Falcon Oast Graphic Art Ltd.

DAVID FICKLING BOOKS
31 Beaumont Street, Oxford, OX1 2NP, UK
a division of RANDOM HOUSE CHILDREN'S BOOKS
61–63 Uxbridge Rd, London W5 5SA
A division of The Random House Group Ltd.

RANDOM HOUSE AUSTRALIA (PTY) LTD
20 Alfred Street, Milsons Point, Sydney,
New South Wales 2061, Australia

RANDOM HOUSE NEW ZEALAND LTD
18 Poland Road, Glenfield, Auckland 10, New Zealand

RANDOM HOUSE (PTY) LTD
Endulini, 5A Jubilee Road, Parktown 2193, South Africa

THE RANDOM HOUSE GROUP Limited Reg. No. 954009
www.kidsatrandomhouse.co.uk

A CIP catalogue record for this book is available from the British Library.

Printed and bound in Great Britain by
Clays Ltd, St Ives plc

To Gwilym and Eleri

Contents

Charming Will

Charming Will

One weekend, the Quigleys went to stay in a nice hotel. They didn't often go to nice hotels. It was a treat.

'What was the last hotel we went to?' Lucy asked as they packed the car on Friday night. 'Was it the one where the crabs escaped from the washbag?'

'No,' Will said. 'It was the one where we played twizzle on the bar seats. Do you remember?'

Dad said, 'I remember both of them very well. I remember the hotel managers coming to talk to me.' Dad reminded them about Good Behaviour. Mum and Dad often talked about Good Behaviour, and how important it was, especially in places like nice hotels. Even at home, the Quigleys had three Family Rules pinned on the toy cupboard door, to help with being well-behaved. The Family Rules were:

1. Be Polite and Pleasant
2. Don't Bicker or Fight
3. Think Before You Speak

'But I'm sure they'll be well-behaved in the hotel,' Mum said. 'They usually are.' She smiled, and they all smiled, and all their smiles were slightly different.

When Will woke the next morning, he noticed to his surprise that his bedroom was much lighter than usual, also much bigger, and the curtains were a completely different

colour. Then he remembered he wasn't in his own room.

He sat up and looked round. The hotel room was big and airy with three large windows and thick windowsills, two easy chairs and a sofa, a television, a desk for writing special hotel postcards and a dressing table with a mirror on it for mums. There was a big bed, where Mum and Dad were still asleep, and another smaller bed with Lucy in it.

'Lucy!' he whispered.

Lucy murmured, 'Wake me up when we get there.'

'Lucy!' he said. 'We're already here! In the hotel! It's morning.'

Lucy sat up and tried to push her eyes round her face with her fingers, and looked at him and then at the room. After she'd yawned, she grinned. 'What are we going to do, Will, now that we're in it?'

Will grinned even more than her. 'We can do whatever we want,' he said. 'That's the point of having a treat in a nice hotel.'

There was a sudden knock on the door, a loud rap, and Lucy squeaked.

Mum and Dad didn't wake up.

'Who's that?' Lucy whispered to Will.

'I don't know,' Will whispered back. He wasn't smiling any more. 'If we're quiet and good, perhaps they'll go away.'

There was another loud rap on the door.

'I don't like that rapping,' Lucy said. 'Make them stop, Will.'

Will got out of bed and went cautiously to the door.

'We haven't done anything wrong,' he said. 'Have we? I haven't. Have you?'

There was a third rap. He opened the

door. A man dressed entirely in black-and-white stripes pushed a trolley past him. 'Good morning, sir,' he said to Will. He parked the trolley in the middle of the room, and retreated. 'Enjoy your breakfast, sir,' he said as he shut the door behind him.

On the trolley were croissants, Danish pastries, warm bread rolls, jams and marmalades, hot and cold milk, orange juice and silver pots of coffee and hot chocolate. Lucy and Will grinned at each other.

'Doing whatever we want,' Will repeated. 'Doing absolutely what we like.'

After the Quigleys had finished their breakfast, and Will had had one Danish pastry too many (eight), and Mum and Lucy had both had three cups of hot chocolate, they all sat about in their pyjamas looking full and talking about what they were going to do for the rest of the day.

'There's a sauna,' Will said. 'And a snooker room. And a croquet pitch. And a ballroom, where I suppose we can play ball games. And a small bar with a darts board. And a big bar with a log fire. And a nice dining room. And a moose head on a wall. It says so in this folder. And we can do whatever we like.'

'So long as you're well-behaved,' Dad said quickly.

'Of course,' Will said. 'You don't need to tell me that.' Will was never badly-behaved, not deliberately anyway, only very, very occasionally, when he sort of forgot the Family Rules.

First, they decided to explore the hotel gardens. Will, who was very excited, led the way. He ran whooping to the staircase, and went down the steps two at a time as far as the bend, where he unexpectedly encountered an elderly man coming up.

8

'Whoops,' he said.

The elderly man recov- ered himself and retrieved his glasses from the wrong part of his face and put them back on his nose. He looked at Will kindly. 'Quite an athlete,' he said. 'What's your name?'

Will felt embarrassed, and mumbled at the floor, and the elderly man pat- ted him on the head and moved on.

Dad wasn't pleased. 'You mustn't go barrelling round corners like that.'

Mum wasn't pleased either. 'Another thing,' she said. 'If someone speaks to you, I expect you to answer properly, Will. It's very rude just to mumble at the floor.'

Will mumbled an apology.

At first the hotel garden was small and colourful, with fancy archways and rose bushes. Then it was big and green, with a wide lawn and a view of hills. Down one side of the lawn there was a row of willows, and, under the willows, a river full of brown shadows and freckly trout. Will said you could catch trout by tickling them, but that didn't work, so he tried telling them jokes instead. Lucy said she saw some of them laughing, but they didn't actually catch any.

It was a sunny morning, and there were quite a few people strolling round the garden. Mum and Dad said good morning to some of them. Lucy said good morning to them

too, but Will was too busy box-
ing with the rose bushes to say
anything. After a while, he got
bored and asked Lucy if she
wanted to explore the hotel
with him.

'Where are you going?'
Mum called after them.

'I'm just going to show
Lucy how to play snooker,'
Will called.

'He doesn't know how to play snooker,'
Dad commented.

'Neither do I,' Mum said, 'so you'd better
go with them.'

On their way to the snooker room, Dad,
Will and Lucy met the elderly gentleman
again, the one Will had barrelled into
earlier.

'Knocked anyone else over?' he said
pleasantly to Will. Will blushed and shuffled
his feet. Out of politeness, Dad stopped to
make conversation. Dad could be very
polite with other people – he made little

noises in his nose and looked keen. But eventually Lucy and Will got bored of watching him and decided to find the snooker room by themselves.

'I don't think Dad will mind,' Will said. 'As long as we're well-behaved.' They went through the big bar with a log fire, past the nice dining room until they came to a book-lined room with an enormous green table in it.

'This is it,' Will said. 'I think.'

Lucy looked round. 'Where's the game? I thought you said snooker was a game.' She looked under the table. 'There's nothing here.'

'This is it,' Will said. 'The table.'

'How do you play it then?'

Will looked vague.

'You don't know, do you?'

'Of course I do.' He looked round for clues. 'It's all to do with getting these coloured balls into the holes at the corners of the table. Somehow.'

Lucy wasn't impressed. 'Anyone can do

that.' She dropped a red ball into a hole.

Will looked round for more clues. 'That's because we haven't got the books out yet,' he said, pointing at the bookshelves.

'What do you do with the books?'

'The books are for making the tracks,' Will said excitedly. 'Tracks on the table for the balls to go down.' Lucy looked at the books. There were lots of them, big and old with gold writing on the thick brown covers. They looked as if they'd been there for hundreds of years.

'Are you sure, Will,' Lucy said. 'They look like the sort of books you're not meant to touch.' But Will was too excited to listen. And in fact, it turned out that the books were very good for building tracks. Will and Lucy piled them up in great wobbly walls and towers, and made mazes and pathways and ramps and tunnels out of them, and sent the balls chugging down them into the holes.

'I like this now, Will,' Lucy said as she finished a slippery pyramid of particularly old books with smooth leather covers and delicate yellowed paper. Will grinned.

'Snooker's a pretty good game,' Will said. 'When you play it properly. Look, here's Shakespeare. I've heard of him, but I never thought he'd make such good hairpin bends. Watch out for those Collected Prayers and Sermons, Lucy, I think they're going to smash onto the floor again.'

Dad came in suddenly, looking for them, and stopped in the doorway, staring at

them with his mouth open.

'Do *you* like snooker, Dad?' Lucy said pleasantly. '*We* like it, and it's only our first go.'

The Quigleys had a late lunch. This was because Dad took the children back to their hotel room first, so he could tell them off without anyone else hearing. He talked for quite a long time about Good Behaviour. He reminded them of the Family Rules at length and quite loudly, and explained that piling up valuable old books on snooker tables counted as Not Being Polite. Will didn't agree, but Dad was very sure. Dad was hoarse from being sure.

★

After lunch, the Quigleys explored the nearby village and bought lollipops, and then it rained so they went back to the hotel and played some board games in the big bar with the log fire, and after that Mum and Dad were tired and they all went up to their room for a rest. Dad was already looking forward to dinner in the nice dining room, but every so often he would say something like, 'But you have to be on your best behaviour,' and give the children a stare. They were funny stares because they made him look surprised, as if he'd just sat on something unexpected.

The children weren't tired at all. While Mum and Dad slumped in the easy chairs, they danced round the room loudly.

'Don't,' Mum said sleepily.

'Why don't you find something to do?' Dad said, yawning.

Will had a good idea. 'Can we go down to the sauna?' he asked, in a very well-mannered voice.

Dad looked uncertain.

'The thing is,' Will said, very politely, 'we know what to do. And what not to do,' he added. He looked as truthful as possible because he thought he might very well have been in a sauna once, though he couldn't quite remember.

Mum and Dad talked about it. Mum had already been down to make sure the sauna was safe for children. Eventually she said it was all right. 'But remember,' she added. 'There might be other people using it, and they won't want to be annoyed. No games.'

Will and Lucy promised no games.

'Nothing unusual with books,' Dad said.

They promised nothing unusual with books.

While Mum and Dad fell asleep, Will and Lucy got ready. They undressed and wrapped towels round their waists, as Mum and Dad had told them to. But when they went out into the corridor they felt shy walking about with just towels on, so they retreated into the room and put on their

pyjamas as well, to be on the safe side.
That made them look funny, so they put
their ordinary clothes over their pyjamas.
Then, feeling pleased and sensible, they left
the room.

'Let's go this way this time,' Will said.

For a while they explored the corridors and landings and little crooked staircases, which all smelled very old and clean. Some of them they explored two or three times, by mistake. And just when they thought they were lost they found themselves at the bottom of the main staircase, looking up at the moose head. It was huge and brown, with an enormous blunt nose, one red glass eye and a black dribble under its chin. Lucy didn't like it, and neither did Will, so they escaped along the hall, shouting things like, 'Did you see it wink?' and 'Is it coming after us?' until they came to a wooden door with SAUNA written on it, and stopped.

'Now listen,' Will said sternly to Lucy. 'This is a sauna and we have to be Polite and Pleasant, and not do things with books, or Dad'll get shouty again, and that's no fun, not even when he does that staring thing so he looks like a rabbit.'

Lucy agreed.

'All right then,' Will said. 'I'll go first.'

JI8I, 336

He pushed open the door, and they went inside.

'Crikey!' he shouted. 'They've got nothing on!'

They stood there staring through a fog of hanging steam. On wooden benches, which ran round the sauna one on top of the other, half a dozen naked people stared back at them.

'Will,' Lucy hissed. 'Be Polite and Pleasant.'

He nodded as politely as he could to the naked people, and they hurried to the end of the lowest bench. He whispered to Lucy, 'Think how much trouble they're all going to be in when the hotel people find out they've been stripping off.'

'What do we do now, Will?'

'Just sit,' Will whispered. 'And don't look.'

'I wasn't looking.'

'Yes you were, I saw you.'

They both looked. The nude people in the sauna were all old – they had large, creased tummies and long, slack arms and knees with dimples like babies. It was an incredible sight and Will and Lucy sat there, open-mouthed, gazing at it all in wonder.

After a while, Lucy's eyes began to prickle and she felt very red-faced.

'Will,' she whispered in a hoarse voice, 'I can't breathe properly.'

'It's probably that second ice cream you ate in the village,' Will said. 'I told you not to have it.'

'No,' Lucy said. 'I'm too hot. And so are

you. Your face is all red.'

Will wiped sweat from his eyes. 'I don't think this sauna's working properly,' he said.

Just then, an old man with a cloudy white chest leaned forward and said, 'If you're feeling too hot, you might want to take off some of your clothes.'

With a shock, Will recognized him as the old man he'd barrelled into that morning. He smiled at him and nodded as politely as he could. 'Don't do it,' he hissed to Lucy. 'We don't want to get told off afterwards.'

'Can't we even take our coats off, Will?' Lucy asked. 'If we fold them neatly on the floor.'

But Will was feeling shyer and shyer. 'I think we should go now,' he whispered. 'I've just remembered, I don't like saunas.'

They got up together. At the door, Will

was overcome by a feeling that he ought to say something, to be polite. He wanted to say that he hoped the sauna got fixed soon, but the sight of all those old naked people made it very hard for him, and in the end he left without saying anything at all.

Mum and Dad were woken by Will and Lucy coming back into the room. It didn't look like Will and Lucy. It looked like two big, boiled parcels coming apart at the seams.

For some time Mum explained to them why going into saunas dressed for Arctic exploration was a bad idea.

'It's not polite either,' Dad said crossly.

'It's not fair,' Will said. 'I'm always trying to be polite, and I'm always being told off for it. How was I to know that they don't play snooker with books here, or that it's OK for really, really old people to strip off and sit around hot and naked?'

Mum decided it was time for a relaxing bath before getting ready for dinner. 'And before we go down,' she added quietly to Dad, 'I think we need another talk with the children. You talk to Lucy and I'll talk to Will.'

Luckily, the bath in their bathroom turned out to be a very relaxing sort of bath. In a wicker basket next to the taps there were little plastic bottles of shampoo and shower gel, and bits of soap wrapped in paper, and a shower cap, and rubbery balls of bath oil, and, though it took a while, Will and Lucy managed to use them all.

Afterwards, Dad talked to Lucy about being well-behaved. She knew he was serious because of the way his eyebrows stayed high up on his forehead all the time. 'There's another thing, Poodle,' he said. 'If we find ourselves chatting with other people in the dining room, you'll be able to chat back, won't you?'

'You mean, "make conversation",' Lucy said.

'Exactly. You know, someone says to you, "Hello, that's a nice dress, is it new?" And you say . . . Well, I don't know what you say to that.' Dad scratched his ear. 'You say something about the dress, I suppose.'

Lucy said, 'I say, "Thank you, that's very kind. It is new, we bought it specially for a nice restaurant like this. But I like what *you're* wearing. Is that new?" Do you mean like that, Dad?'

Dad didn't say anything, he just patted her head.

'That's nothing, Dad,' Lucy said. 'I could have a much longer conversation than that. I'll teach you if you like,' she added kindly.

In the meantime, Mum talked to Will. After a while he promised not to shout, jump, or pull the face of the Mad Troll of the Toilet.

'And if we meet anyone, Will, and start talking to them, what will you do?'

'Be quiet so that other people can hear properly,' he said promptly.

'No, Will. If they talk to you, you'll make conversation, won't you?'

'But I won't know them.'

'You could think of interesting things to tell them. Like what you're doing at school.'

He looked puzzled. 'You mean if they're teachers and want to get ideas for their lessons?'

Mum explained that all sorts of people might be interested about what Will did at school. 'And after you've told them some things about yourself, what might you say next?'

Will was stumped.

'Maybe you could ask them some questions about themselves?'

'Oh no,' he said, shocked. 'That would be nosy.'

Mum sighed and began again, and at long last, Will got the idea of making conversation and went into a corner of the room to practise by himself. The others could hear him saying things like, 'What do you think of wigs?' and 'I don't suppose you like reptiles, do you?'

At last, they were all ready for dinner.

'It's been a good weekend,' Dad said, as they went down the stairs to the dining room. 'Mostly. And this is going to be the best bit of it.'

The dining room was very pretty with pink tablecloths and vases of carnations, and all the Quigleys were impressed. There was something else about it too: it was very quiet, as if everyone was on their very best behaviour.

Their starters came, and they ate them hungrily. Dad had frogs' legs, which everyone else said was shocking, even after they'd all tried them and Will had tried them four or five times.

As they were finishing their starters, the old man from the sauna sat down at the table next to them and began to chat. He winked at Will, and Will felt tongue-tied again. He asked Will if he was enjoying himself at the hotel, and Will nodded and couldn't think of anything to say, and Lucy helped him with his conversation by saying that she'd enjoyed everything about it except the moose head, the sauna and the snooker table before it had books on it, carefully describing the ways in which she disliked these things.

'But really we're enjoying our weekend very much,' Mum said. 'Aren't we, Will?'

Will nodded briefly. 'When are they bringing the next course?' he asked.

Their main courses arrived very soon. Everyone had a bit of everyone else's, and they carried on talking. Lucy told the old man about the laughing fish in the river.

'They did look funny, didn't they, Will?' Mum said.

This time, Will was too busy eating to answer. He gave a small grunt to show that he'd heard the question and understood it. The food was extremely good, and when he wasn't eating, he was sitting feeling full and smiling at the tablecloth. As soon as the puddings arrived, he tucked in immediately.

He had chosen four special sorts of ice cream all piled together with crunchy toffee casing and chocolate sauce. Before Mum could stop him, he lifted up the bowl to his face and licked it clean, and sat back with a slight accidental burp.

It was only then that he noticed Mum's expression. Dad's expression wasn't very good either. At first he didn't know what the expressions meant. He checked his shirt to see if he'd spilled

anything big on it, but he hadn't. Then, at
last, he remembered about making conversation.

Partly because he wanted to show Mum
and Dad how polite he could be, and partly
because he was feeling so good after the
wonderful dinner, he decided he would give
it a go, and, without wasting any more
time, said suddenly, 'Last week we saw this
film at school about health and safety.' He
spoke very clearly so the old man at the
next table could hear. He was pleased to see
that the man stopped what he was saying
and looked interested. So did some of the
people at other tables, who turned round to
look at him.

'That's interesting, Will,' Mum said encouragingly. 'You don't have to speak quite so loudly though.'

Now that he'd made a beginning, Will went on confidently. 'Anyway, in this film there was this man, and he went across some railway tracks to get to the other side, and he slipped and fell onto the electric rail.'

The dining room grew hushed as other people listened to Will.

'A bit quieter,' Mum said to him in a low voice.

'He fell face down on the tracks,' Will went on in the same forthright style. 'And his head cooked from the inside, and his skin melted and ran off his face in a hot puddle.'

It was very quiet in the dining room now. Many people had stopped eating and sat staring at their plates. Will was pleased by the dramatic effect of his story. 'That wasn't the worst accident, though,' he said, now deliberately addressing the whole dining room. 'There was this other man who got onto the tracks to put a coin on them, and got his coat sleeve stuck.'

'Enough, Will,' Dad whispered.

'All they found of him,' Will continued enthusiastically, 'was his feet and the stumps of his legs. And guess what? They were still steaming.'

The dining room was now completely silent. A lady got up and left, holding a hand to her mouth. 'Then there was the other man,' Will went on, enthusiastically.

Dad said, 'No more, Will.' His voice was very firm. His face was firm too, and rather red.

'I was only making conversation,' Will said, crestfallen.

'Well, don't,' Dad hissed.

'But you said I had to.'

'Try to think of something else to talk about,' Mum said calmly. 'Tell us about some of the other things you're doing at school. What was that project you were doing in History?'

'The Victorians,' Will said shortly. The Victorians weren't nearly as interesting as grisly railway accidents.

'Good,' Mum said. 'Tell us about the Victorians.'

Will started off slowly and reluctantly. After a while he got on to everyday life in Victorian London. 'It was pretty rotten because everything was so filthy,' he said. 'People were always dying of diseases. Like cholera. Cholera's a really bad disease,' he said, perking up again. Dad was looking at him funnily, but he ignored him. 'Do you know where the word "cholera" comes from?' he asked. The old man shook his head. 'It's Greek for diarrhoea.' Will was very pleased to have remembered this, and, though he noticed Dad signalling to him widly with his eyebrows, he went on with passion, 'It was horrible, all the hospitals were full of people with cholera, and everything was filthy and the toilets were all overflowing, and there was diarrhoea everywhere. In this one hospital there was this nurse, and she'd had a long, hard day, and she sat down to drink a cup of tea. And it wasn't tea. Do you know what it was that she drank? Can you guess?'

'Stop now,' Dad yelled abruptly.

Will stopped and looked at Dad. Dad's face was a funny colour. He looked at Mum. Her face was a funny colour too. Then he looked round the room.

Half the people were staring at the tablecloths on their tables, and half of them were staring at Will. No one was making a sound.

It dawned on him that he was the cause of all this silence.

Dad began to hiss something under his breath. It was difficult to hear what he was saying because his voice was so quiet and so very, very cross, and all the words sounded as if they had been bitten in half. But Will knew he was in trouble. He knew he had to do something quickly, but he couldn't think what.

At that moment, their waiter came to take away their empty pudding bowls, and suddenly Will knew. 'Excuse me,' he said. 'I'd like to speak to the person who does all the food here.'

The waiter nodded and disappeared.

Dad's eyebrows were now so high on his head, they looked as if they were trying to escape into his hair. 'Will! Whatever it is you're going to do, please don't . . .'

But it was too late. A large man with a long moustache dressed as a baker came heavily through the dining room, and stopped at the Quigleys' table. He didn't look very pleased to be there.

'Yes?' he said curtly with a strong foreign accent.

Will glanced over at Mum and Dad, who were looking at him in horror. Everyone else in the dining room was also looking at him in horror, wondering what the boy with the loud voice and disgusting stories was going to say now. He felt very nervous, but he stood up so everyone could hear him better, and spoke loudly and clearly.

'I just want to say that this dinner was

the best dinner I've ever eaten,' he said.
'Really brilliant. And my mum's a pretty
good cook, and she's sitting there, so you
can tell I mean it.'

The dining room was still silent after he
said this, but the silence was softer somehow. Will felt a little bolder.

'The ice cream pudding was especially
brilliant. You know, the thing with the
chocolate sauce. That was the most . . .' He
searched for the right word. 'The most . . .
exquisite, the most . . .' He tried to think of

something even better. 'The most . . . luscious, the most . . .' He racked his brains till his eyes bulged. 'The most deliciousest thing I've ever eaten. Ever.'

The silence in the dining room softened quite a bit more after this. 'Hear, hear,' someone said.

'That's right,' Will said. 'I don't suppose I'll ever forget it, that pudding, all my life. And I'm only nine,' he added.

He was about to sit down, when the large man with the moustache, who had been listening to him seriously, suddenly seized him by the hand.

'I too,' he said, 'would like to say something.' He turned slightly to address the whole dining room. 'All my life,' he said, 'this is why I cook. To give the pleasure.' He turned back to Will and gave a slight bow. 'You, *monsieur,* are the most charming person I have ever cooked for, and I thank you.'

There was no more silence in the dining room. Instead, there was a lot of murmuring, and some light, appreciative applause, which echoed round as the Quigleys left their table and quickly made their way out of the room.

That night the Quigleys all lay together in Mum and Dad's bed, falling asleep.

'I'm so tired,' Mum said with a yawn.

'It's the excitement,' Dad said. 'The excitement of not knowing what he was going to say next.'

'But he was Polite and Pleasant,' Lucy reminded them. 'In the end.'

'Not polite,' Will murmured sleepily. 'Charming!' And then he was asleep. And though he was asleep, he was still grinning.

Clever Lucy

Clever Lucy

Every week, Lucy and Will got pocket money. They were very interested in pocket money. This was because they were always saving up to buy something. What they were saving up for changed all the time. First, Lucy was saving up for a puppet theatre, then for a clown costume, then a jewellery box. Will changed his mind even more. One day he'd say, 'How much do security cameras cost, Mum?' and the next he'd be asking Dad where you could buy a decent flock of goats.

Mum and Dad saved up for things too, but the things they saved up for were boring, like electricity bills and car repairs. Most of the time they complained that they didn't have enough money.

One afternoon, Lucy went into the back room to find Mum and Dad sitting at the table, talking. They were talking in a very serious way. They were talking so seriously they didn't hear Lucy come in. Lucy stayed there for a while, politely listening to them, then went upstairs to find Will.

Will was in their bedroom making a model of a goat out of cereal boxes. 'I definitely think we should get some goats,' he said, when she came in. 'Don't you, Lucy? In the Old Testament just about everyone owns a goat.'

Lucy said, 'Will, you know how Mum and Dad are always going on about money?'

'It's terrible, isn't it?' Will said. 'I don't know what we're going to do about it.'

'Well, Dad says we're really poor this year. Because of tacks.'

'What sort of tacks?'

Lucy shrugged. 'Just tacks. Must be lots of them,' she added.

Will stopped making his goat and looked

sad. 'I don't suppose they'll be interested in helping out with my flock then,' he said heavily.

'It's worse than that, Will. Mum says we might not even be able to have any more treats.'

Will looked scared.

'What shall we do, Will?'

They sat on the carpet, thinking.

'How much money do you have in your piggy bank?' Will asked.

Lucy counted it out. 'Twenty five pence and an IOU note from Mum for five pounds. What about you?'

'Not nearly so much as that,' Will said gloomily.

They sat together staring at the carpet in silence. It was a nice carpet but it was full of socks.

Lucy said, 'We need to get some more money, to give to Mum and Dad.'

'I know,' Will said. 'And it has to be quite a lot of money, because the things they like to buy are expensive, even though they're so boring. We need a plan. An expensive plan. Wait! I know.'

'What?'

'Jobs round the house. Mum and Dad are always asking us to do things round the house, and usually we don't bother, but now we can do them, and they can pay us. I bet they'll even be pleased.'

They tried to ask Dad about jobs, but he said he was too busy, and he went upstairs very fast, looking distracted.

Mum explained that Dad was filling in a form called a tax return. 'It's a very complicated form,' she said. 'I don't know if

Dad can do it right,' she added.

'What sort of tacks?' Will asked.

Mum explained that tax was money you gave to the government.

Will and Lucy didn't like the sound of giving money away, and said so, and Mum started to explain again.

'Yeah, yeah,' Will said. 'You're always going on about money, Mum.' He used a friendly voice so she'd know he wasn't being rude.

Lucy asked if they could do jobs round the house, and Mum said she'd be very pleased if they cleaned the car.

'Told you,' Will whispered to Lucy. 'It's going to be easy getting money for all those tacks.'

They went outside to the car. 'Which bits need doing?' Will said in a business-like voice.

Mum showed him.

'That's all of it,' he said, shocked. 'I thought perhaps some bits wouldn't need doing. It'll be a lot of work doing all of it.'

Mum said that after they finished the outside of the car, they should do the inside.

Will made a face. 'The inside as well?'

'And I'll give you five pounds.'

'Five pounds for the outside?'

'No. Five pounds for the outside and the inside.'

Will made another face, even madder. 'But it'll take us hours to do all that. Days.

We could be weeks doing nothing but cleaning this car.' He couldn't think of anything else to say, he was too outraged. He turned and went back into the house.

'Sorry, Mum,' Lucy said. She whispered, 'We'll come back and do it when we aren't doing such an expensive plan.'

Mum laughed. 'What plan's that?'

'It's a we-need-a-lot-of-money plan.'

Mum sighed. 'You two. You're always going on about money.'

Now that their first plan had failed, Will and Lucy had to think of another one. First plans can be quite easy to think of, but second plans are harder. Some people get too tired to think of a second plan at all. But Will and Lucy never gave up after just one plan.

Will said, 'We need a plan that's nothing to do with mums and dads. That's important, because they take up too much time for not enough money.'

'A secret plan,' Lucy said.

'Yes.'

'And a surprise plan. Because when we give all that money to Mum and Dad, they'll be surprised.' She smiled at the

51

thought of this.

They sat on the carpet, trying to think of secret, surprising plans. They sat there for so long that after a while Lucy discovered she'd made a small camel out of all the spare socks. But she still didn't give up thinking.

At last, Will said, 'Have you thought of a plan yet?'

'I think so.'

'I think I have too. First we'll talk about yours, then we'll talk about mine. But remember, we have to keep them secret.'

A few days later, Dad was walking Will and Lucy to school. When they reached the end of the street, a large object fell out of Will's school bag onto the pavement.

'What have you got there, Will?' Dad said.

'Nothing,' he said, quickly shoving it up his jumper.

Dad took it off him. It was a two-litre bottle of budget cola. Dad looked baffled.

'What on earth are you taking this to school for?'

Will looked shifty. 'It'll be useful if I get thirsty.'

Dad stopped looking baffled and looked shocked instead. 'Two litres of it? You'll do your bladder a mischief.'

'Well, other people will help me drink it.'

'What people?'

'Anyone who'll pay.' As soon as he said this, Will wished he hadn't. Now Dad had the squeezed look. Dad's squeezed look usually meant that Will had to start explaining himself.

Will started explaining that he'd been buying cheap cola in very large bottles and selling it in quite small, not-so-cheap cupfuls to thirsty children in the playground at break.

'Thirty pence for a full cup, twenty for half a cup, and fifteen for a dribble at the bottom.'

'And people actually buy it from you?' Dad spluttered. 'Even though they know it's expensive rubbish.'

'Oh yes, they like expensive rubbish.'

'And you're allowed to sell things at school, are you?'

Will wasn't sure about that, so he said, very carefully and truthfully, that no one had asked him to stop. He didn't mention that he sold the cola at the far side of the playing field, round the back of the old willow, where he couldn't be seen.

Dad was confused. His squeezed look vanished and was replaced by his distracted

one. 'I still don't understand why you're doing it.'

'To make money'

'But what for?'

Will opened his mouth, but before he could speak, Lucy said quickly, 'He can't say. It's a secret.'

'Oh yeah,' Will said sheepishly. 'Nearly forgot. It's a cunning plan, but it's secret, and Lucy agrees, so we can't tell you. But don't worry. It isn't a bad secret. It's a good one.' He winked at Dad. 'You'll like it.'

Dad didn't agree. Will and Dad had an argument. Dad said he didn't like Will selling things at school, and Will said there was nothing wrong with it, especially because of the reason he was doing it, which was a secret of the good sort, and Dad suggested they go and ask Miss Strickland, the head teacher, what she thought of it, and Will didn't say anything to that at first, and then he explained for quite a long time why it wasn't fair. Then finally he said, in a quiet sort of voice, that he supposed he wouldn't do it again.

As they went into school, Will said to Lucy, 'Well, that didn't work. You'll have to try your plan now.'

Lucy nodded. 'I've got my things ready,' she said.

At lunchtime, Will saw Lucy hurrying past the door to the new block, and asked her how it was going.

'I can't stop,' she said. 'I've got six of them waiting for me in the music practice room.'

In the room, she found Pokehead getting the girls into an orderly line.

'Nearly ready,' Pokehead said. 'They've all written their names in the book, and what they want doing.'

'That's good,' Lucy said. She was glad Pokehead was helping her. When Pokehead asked people to do something they generally did it. She sat down at the desk and got her

things out. 'I'm ready now,'
she said.

The girl at the front of
the line came forward
and stood by the desk.
Her name was Mary,
but her friends called her
Memu, and some of her
friends called her Moo.

'What do you want,
Moo?' Lucy asked.

'I want the big one,'
Moo said.

'Really?'

Moo nodded.

'Where do you want it?'

Moo pointed. 'All the
way across here.'

'Are you sure?'

Moo nodded again.
'And I want it in orange
and purple.'

Lucy checked the felt-
tips in her pencil case.

'It'll cost you,' Pokehead said to Mary.

'That's all right, I'll get the money from my mum.'

'It'll take me a long time to do something that big,' Lucy said. Pokehead looked at the other girls.

'We don't mind waiting,' they said. 'We want to see Lucy do it.'

'That's all right then,' Lucy said. She turned to Mary. 'OK, Moo. First you have to take your top off and then you have to lie down on the desk.'

Later that day, as Lucy and Will were getting out of the bath, Mum called Lucy down. She twisted her wet hair into a towel, as Mum had shown her, and put on her pyjamas and dressing gown, and went downstairs. She was feeling pleased with herself.

But Mum wasn't pleased with her. 'I've just had a phone call from Mary's mum,' she said.

Lucy felt shy suddenly.

'Do you know what it was about?'

Lucy didn't know whether to nod or shake her head, so she kept it very still, looking up at Mum.

'She rang to complain,' Mum said. 'Because Mary came home this afternoon and asked her for ten pounds to pay for a picture in orange and purple felt-tip of a five-legged cow which you drew, apparently, across both her shoulders. Is that true?'

Lucy finally nodded. 'She did ask me to, though.'

Mum frowned and made a cross noise.

Mum's cross noise sounded like the end of a shout, and Lucy didn't like it. Then Mum got Lucy's spelling book out of her reading folder.

'At the back of this book, there's a list of names and numbers and other odd things,' she said. ' "Inez: face, 5. Gilly: hand, 3. Ellie: two hands and one foot, 7".' She looked sternly at Lucy. 'You've been doing pictures of cows on people for money, haven't you?' she said.

'One cow,' Lucy said. 'And three trolls. And a pig. But the pig had to have wings,' she added, 'so it cost more.'

Mum stared at her. 'Why did you do it?'

Lucy shook her head. 'I can't tell you. It's a secret and a surprise.'

Mum was cross. 'I don't like you being so interested in money all the time,' she said. 'It's not right. It's greedy.' And she sent Lucy back upstairs.

Lucy and Will lay in bed talking sadly about money. They had made hardly any

60

money from selling things at school, and they were glum. They knew that if second and third plans are difficult to think up, fourth plans are even harder. Many children give up. But Will and Lucy didn't like giving up, and they were never glum for long. Lucy was too hopeful to be glum, and Will was too cunning.

'Be quiet a minute now, Lucy,' Will said. 'I'm going to think.'

He thought about Mum and Dad telling them they weren't allowed to make money at school anymore, and what that meant.

After a while he sat up in bed. 'It means we are allowed to make money in other places,' he said out loud.

'What places, Will?'

Will wasn't listening. He was still thinking, and he sat there chewing his bottom lip, looking cunning. 'I've got it!' he said at last. 'I've got a fourth plan. A street sale!'

Lucy sat up too and clapped her hands. 'We can sell lots of stuff at a street sale. I can sell my doll's house. It would be easy for someone to mend.'

'And I could sell my mini-bugs thousand-piece jigsaw, because there's only a handful of pieces missing.'

'And that scratchy shirt I have to wear for best.'

'And the nit comb, because it hurts.'

'And the ordinary combs because they all hurt too.'

'And my maths test cards because they're too hard.'

'And all those vitamin pills we have to

take that taste horrid. There are lots of things we could sell.'

'I like street sales,' Lucy said.

Will grinned in the dark. 'So do I. And this is going to be the biggest and best street sale ever. That sounds good,' he added. 'I think we should put it on the poster.'

On Saturday morning, Mum and Dad went shopping while Will and Lucy played at Elizabeth, Timothy and Pokehead's. Before they went into town, Dad helped the children take playthings over to their friends' house.

'What a lot of bags,' he panted. 'What's in them?'

'Toys,' Will said. 'And stuff like that.'

'Well, see you later,' Dad said. 'Be good.'

At lunchtime, Mum and Dad came back from town. They walked down the street. 'Look,' Dad said. 'There's a crowd of

people outside our house. I wonder what they're doing.'

'I can see Will and Lucy,' Mum said. 'Standing behind that table.'

Dad frowned. 'It looks like our table.'

They walked on a bit more, and saw a poster stuck to a lamppost. 'Someone's having a street sale,' Dad said. 'Listen to this. *Biggest, Best Street Sale Ever. Nearly Perfect Toys. Best Shirts Hardly Worn. Health Things Like Nit Combs.*'

'Sounds good,' Mum said. 'Perhaps we could go. Where is it?'

Dad made a noise. It was the same noise he made whenever he banged his knee on the table leg. 'Quick!' he shouted. 'Run! Perhaps they haven't sold it all yet!'

After Mum and Dad had made them buy back all their old nit combs and maths test cards, Will and Lucy lay in bed after lights out, talking about money again.

'I didn't realize how hard it is to make,' Lucy said sadly. 'It's very hard to make even a little bit. How much do we have now, Will?'

'Nothing,' Will said. 'Actually, a bit less than nothing, because I had to buy back my jigsaw from Tim for more than he paid for it.'

'He can be like that, Tim,' Lucy said.

They thought about Tim for a while. Then they thought about money again.

'I hate having used up all my ideas,' Will said. 'It makes me feel sticky.'

'How many plans have we had?' Lucy asked.

'Four.'

That made them feel sadder, because hardly anyone thinks of fifth plans – they're usually far too tired by then.

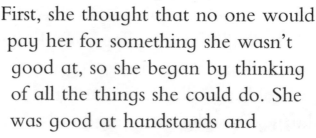

They lay in bed thinking. Lucy tried hard not to have used up all her ideas. First, she thought that no one would pay her for something she wasn't good at, so she began by thinking of all the things she could do. She was good at handstands and cartwheels. She was good at remembering people's names. She was very good at pictures of five-legged cows and trolls and flying pigs. From the bunk above she could hear Will breathing deeply as if he were already asleep, but she went on thinking. Would people pay her for remembering names for them? Would people pay to watch her doing her best cartwheels? She didn't think so. Then she suddenly sat up.

'Will!' she whispered loudly.

He woke up with a snort, saying, 'Wasn't me, I never touched it.'

'Will,' Lucy said. 'I haven't used up all my ideas. I've got one left.'

'What idea?'

'Doing a show! We're always doing shows, and we're good at them, and people pay to see shows, don't they, Will?'

Lucy lay perfectly still in the bottom bunk, grinning to herself in the dark and waiting to hear what Will would say. After a while she heard him breathing deeply again. She didn't wake him. She lay in bed and quietly thought about the show. Though she was tired, she wanted to think of everything before she fell asleep. In her mind, she had a picture of it. They were in the front room, with a big curtain hung across the middle so they could change costumes on one side and come onto the stage on the other. Elizabeth, Timothy and Pokehead were in it too, dressed up in armour, and they had coloured flags and musical instruments, and Pokehead had big animal ears on. Sometimes they were saying their lines, and sometimes they were dancing, and sometimes they were doing a fight, but Lucy couldn't quite guess what the show was. She wished she knew, but she was getting sleepier and sleepier, and as she fell asleep she wondered sadly if she'd have forgotten it all in the morning when she woke up.

But she hadn't. Will woke up to find Lucy's face an inch away from his own, saying, 'Will, wake up, we're going to do a

show. And people will pay to see it. And the show's going to be *The Lion, the Witch and the Wardrobe.*'

On the morning of the show, Lucy rehearsed everyone one last time. Will was Peter, Mr Beaver and the musical accompaniment. Lucy was Lucy, which she thought was very convenient. Elizabeth was Aslan. Tim was Edmund and Mr Tumnus. And Pokehead was the Old Professor, the Fat Dwarf, the White Witch and Mrs Beaver. Fatbrain, the Peachey's cat, was a wolf, though most of the time he was just a cat, and more often than not a sleeping cat. All the other parts were to be shared by Lucy and Pokehead as necessary. And, of course, Lucy was the director of the show.

'Good, Will,' she said, as they practised. 'Try to smile when you kill the wolf.'

'I can't kill it,' Will said. 'I can't even wake it up.'

They'd hung a sheet across the middle of the Quigleys' front room to act as a curtain. The stage side was decorated with paintings of trees and animals and snow. The back-stage side was full of armour, ribbons, wands, blood capsules, false ears and a clarinet.

'Is the audience ready?' Lucy asked. They looked through the crack in the curtain. Sitting in the front room were Mum and Dad, Ben and Philippa; Lucy's friends Ellie, Gilly, Mary and Inez; and Will's friends Matt, Dani and Sandy.

'We ought to have some fresh mints to sell at half-time,' Lucy said thoughtfully.

'What fresh mints?' asked Tim, who liked mints.

'You always have fresh mints at shows,' Lucy explained. 'Usually there's a man with a tray selling them, and he shouts out, "Fresh mints! Fresh mints!" so you know to go and buy them.'

'Don't you mean "refreshments"?' Elizabeth asked.

This took Lucy by surprise. But it was her show after all. 'Some shows have refreshments, but my shows have fresh

mints,' she said firmly.

The show began. At first it went well, and the audience liked it very much. When it snowed in Narnia, Will threw handfuls of washing powder over the top of the curtain, and hardly anybody sneezed and the snow smelled very clean. The audience clapped admiringly.

Lucy was very good as Lucy, and Tim, who was wearing toilet rolls on his head, was a surprisingly good faun, except when he had to cry. He reluctantly made a short barking noise like a seal, and said to the audience, 'I'm not really crying, I never cry, I haven't cried since I was three.' The audience applauded respectfully.

In quiet moments, when the actors were changing costumes or whispering instructions to each other, Fatbrain could be seen quietly destroying parts of the hanging sheet, to the intense delight of the boys in the audience. But there weren't many quiet bits. Pokehead was a very fierce White Witch, and said lots of things she didn't

usually have chance to say, like "This may wreck all" and "I see you are an idiot", which she said to Tim (who was now playing Edmund) much more than she actually needed to. When Pokehead asked him what he would like to eat, he got his own back by asking for fresh mints instead of Turkish Delight, and things were confused for a while, but she saved the scene by making an unexpected change into the Fat Dwarf, wrapping herself in a duvet and bouncing around the stage off the front room walls. After they'd managed to get out of her way, the audience cheered.

There was a slightly boring bit at the Beaver's lodge, where Will, who was both Peter and Mr Beaver, had a long conversation with himself. But there were some terrifically good bits after that, with

Aslan, majestically played by Elizabeth in a fluffy blonde wig, orange pyjamas and high heel shoes. They'd all learned their lines very well, and if they couldn't quite remember the right word, they used a word that sounded very similar, so no one would notice.

'Let Aslan be nozzled!' the White Witch commanded.

'Muzzled,' Aslan whispered.

'You can be muzzled after you've been nozzled,' Pokehead said sternly.

Nothing went seriously wrong until the final battle at the end, when the White Witch caused an upset by decisively defeating Aslan. For a few seconds, no one quite knew what to do. Edmund and Peter, who had a whole bottle of ketchup to use, were too busy being injured even to notice what had happened. But Lucy and Pokehead saved the day with the brilliant idea of running through all their parts very fast one last time, becoming, in quick succession, Mrs Macready, a Pelican, several

Boggles and Ogres, the Old Professor, a
Unicorn, a Horde of Mice, some Wraiths, a
Horror, the Giant Rumblebuffin, and finally,
the Fat Dwarf, who bounced onto stage
again to great cheers from the audience.
Unfortunately, not being able to see where
he was going because of his amazing fat-
ness, the Fat Dwarf accidentally trod on
Fatbrain. At once, Fatbrain was transformed
from a sleeping cat into a wolf, which is
what he should have been all along, and in
a wonderful display of wolfishness he utterly
destroyed the curtain, which fell in a heap
on top of everyone. From underneath, Lucy
could be heard shouting, 'The end! Please
help!' And the audience rose cheering to its
feet.

Afterwards, the Quigleys sat in the back
room talking about it.

'Did you really like it, Mum?' Lucy
asked, for the seventh time.

'Everyone loved it,' she said. 'Didn't you
see us cheering?'

'I did until I fell under the sheet. What was your best bit?'

'Well, I liked the nozzling of Aslan very much. And Tim's fresh mints.'

Lucy smiled shyly. 'I liked those bits too. Didn't you, Will?'

Will didn't answer. He was sitting glumly at the table with a pen and paper.

Mum said, 'What's the matter, Will? Didn't you enjoy the show?'

'It's not the show,' he said. 'It's the money from the show. We hardly made anything.'

'How much did you think you'd make?'

'A few hundred pounds.'

'Oh. And what did you actually get?'

'Four pounds fifty, ten Bolivian pesos, a car wash token, a raffle ticket from last year's school fête and some used bubble gum.'

Dad began to say that shows are more important

than the money you make from them, and
Mum began to say that she wished they
wouldn't think about money all the time,
when Will interrupted. 'Go on, Lucy,' he
said. 'It was your fifth plan, so you'd better
give it.'

Mum and Dad looked at each other.

Lucy made a pile of the money and
things from the show, and gave it to Dad,
and did a little curtsey. 'It's for you and
Mum,' she said. 'From me and Will.
Because of being poor this year with all
those tacks.'

Dad stared at it.

'Is that what you've been doing all this
time?' Mum said. 'Was the money always
going to be for us?'

'All of it,' Lucy said. 'Really. And the car
wash token.'

'And the bubble gum,' Will said. 'It's only got a few toothmarks in it.'

Dad gave an embarrassed grin. He scratched an ear and coughed. They all looked at him.

'This is very nice,' he said. 'Very, very nice. And I know I thought we were going to be really poor this year,' he said. 'But, you see' – he scratched his ears a lot more – 'I made a mistake.'

'What sort of mistake?'

'A mistake with my tax.'

'Was it a bad mistake?'

'No, it was a good one. I got all my

sums wrong on my tax form. It turns out I don't have to pay money to the tax people after all. In fact,' he added, 'they have to pay a bit of money to me.'

Everyone, including Mum, looked at Dad. 'Sorry,' he said. 'You see, it was just too complicated.'

'In that case,' Will said, 'can I have the bubble gum back?'

'In that case,' Lucy said, 'does it mean we can have treats after all?'

Dad nodded. They all cheered.

'And does it mean,' Will said, with his mouth full of second-hand bubble gum, 'that we needn't have spent hours and hours thinking up plan after plan after plan?'

'I liked our plans,' Lucy said.

Will thought for a bit. 'So did I,' he said. He became cheerful again. 'It's odd, isn't it, how plans work. Sometimes they're very straightforward, and sometimes they're all twisty.'

'I don't mind twisty ones,' Lucy said.

'Neither do I,' Will said. He looked at

Mum and Dad thoughtfully.

'I wonder if they work with flocks of goats,' he said.

Out with Mum

Out With Mum

On Mother's Day morning, Lucy and Will got up early and made breakfast for Mum. They did sugar bread under the grill and cut it into slices, and spread hot cross buns with chocolate spread, and poured orange juice into one of the glasses that didn't have a crack in it. They got their presents and cards and an interesting twig in a vase for decoration, and put them all on a tray, which Lucy sprinkled with coloured sequins from her party kit to make it more Mother's Day-ish.

They were very proud of Mum's Mother's Day breakfast. They carried it up to Mum and Dad's room, and put it on top of her and got into bed beside her to help her eat it.

'Happy Mother's Day, Mum,' Lucy said.
'Happy Mother's Day, Mum,' Will said.
'What time is it?' Mum groaned.
'Not that early,' Will said. 'It'll be getting light soon. What are you going to eat first, Lucy?'

'Sugar bread.'

'I'm going to have a hot cross bun. Come on, Mum. You have to wake up and start eating or there won't be any left.'

After breakfast, the Quigleys went downstairs to laze in their pyjamas and discuss what to do for the rest of the day. Dawn had broken, and it was going to be a fine Saturday.

'It's Mum's choice,' Lucy said kindly. 'What do you want to do, Mum? You can choose anything you like.'

'I'd like to go for a walk.'

'Except a walk,' Lucy said quickly.

'Too late,' Dad said.

'But we hate walks,' Lucy said. It was true. Neither Will nor Lucy could understand them. They could understand walking home from school, which was a tired but pleasant sort of walk, they could understand walking to the sweet shop, which was an excited, impatient walk, but walking *for the sake of walking* they couldn't understand at all.

'What's the point of that?' Will said. 'It's so boring.'

Dad explained what a good day it would be if they all went for a walk in the countryside, then came home for a nice Mother's Day dinner in the evening.

'That would be a rotten day,' Will said frankly.

Dad explained a bit more loudly that because it was Mother's Day it was naturally Mum's choice to do what she wanted. 'So let's have no more arguing,' he said.

'I'm not *arguing*,' Will said. 'I'm just saying we don't want to go.'

'You are arguing,' Dad said.

'No, I'm not.'

'You are.'

'I'm not.'

After Will had spent quite a lot of time proving he wasn't arguing, the Quigleys set

out on Mum's Mother's Day walk. They
went down their street, Will and Lucy at
the front, Mum in the middle, and Dad last,
bent under the weight of a large rucksack.

'Tell me again what's in this rucksack,'
he said.

'Just some snacks and things,' Mum said.

'And some *Beanos*,' Will said. 'For when we get bored walking.'

'And some colouring things and puzzles,' Lucy said. 'For when we get bored with the *Beanos*.'

'Oh, and some board games,' Will added.

'And the collection of stones from our last walk,' Lucy said.

All their raincoats were in the rucksack too. So were four bottles of water, a first-aid kit, some maps, walk books and guides to birds and wild flowers.

Dad groaned. 'Well, do we really need the stones?' he said.

The children said you never knew when you might need some stones.

At the end of the street, they turned into the cycle track. Now Mum was at the front and Will and Lucy were in the middle. Dad was still at the back. Lucy gave Dad her skipping rope and Frisbee to put in the rucksack, and Will gave Dad his safari hat and combat jacket. It was a warm day, and

a few minutes later he gave Dad his red
football jersey too, but Dad gave it back to
him.

At the end of the cycle track, Mum was
still at the front but now Dad was in the
middle, and Will and Lucy were last. Mum
gave out the first of the boiled sweets that
she used for encouraging Will and Lucy on
walks. Then they crossed the lake, went
over the railway lines, and came out into
the countryside.

'Is it time for our picnic now?' Lucy asked
in a tired voice.

Mum looked at her watch. 'How long do
you think we've been walking?' she asked.
'Roughly.'

Lucy thought. 'An hour? An hour and a half?'

'Eleven minutes,' Mum said.

'Oh.'

They set off again.

'Have we got much further to go?' Will called wearily.

'Yes,' Mum said, without turning round. Will waited for her to say something else, but she didn't.

Lucy looked across the yellow and green fields stretching in front of her, and her heart sank. Everything was so big, and it took so long to get from one side of it to the other. It was all right for Mum and Dad, they didn't mind fields, they liked them. They walked across them quickly, saying things like, 'Look at the hawthorns!' and 'Did you hear that pheasant?' while Will and Lucy lagged behind glumly.

Will got himself a stick and began to

beat a hedge. Lucy got herself a stick too,
but it was too thick and slow to beat hedges
with and she threw it away in disgust.

After a little while she sat on the grass
and wouldn't move.

'What's wrong, Poodle?' Dad said.

'It hurts.'

'A stone in your shoe?'

'No, the walk.'

Dad said he would play a game, and
Lucy cheered up a bit. First they played
tracking. Dad went ahead through the
woods and left arrows on the ground which
Will and Lucy had to find. Dad made the
arrows out of stones, grass, flowerheads,

mud and sheaves of barley which he shouldn't have taken from the farmer's field. Will and Lucy found them all.

Then it was Will and Lucy's turn. They made arrows out of dust, part of a tree, a bend in a country road and some sheep. Even though he took a long time, Dad didn't find any of them.

'Right,' he said. 'If you want to be tricky, I can be tricky too.'

He went off again, quite fast, with the fat rucksack jumping on his back, and a short while later the children found him being told off in someone's garden. A man in a hat was saying, 'I don't want people coming into my garden, even if it is to do something as stupid as make shapes out of my lawn clippings.'

After that, the Quigleys stopped for a rest and some snacks.

'Well,' Mum said. 'You see how nice a walk can be?'

Lucy scowled.

Will said, 'The only good bit so far was when Dad got told off by that man with the hat.'

They went on with their walk. Soon Will and Lucy got bored again, and Mum agreed to play the hiding game. First Lucy ran ahead and hid, and the others came after, trying to spot her before she jumped out at them with a terrifying squeak. Next, Mum went ahead. The others followed and went round a corner just in time to see her spring loudly out of a hedge into the path of two elderly ladies in headscarves.

After this they stopped playing games altogether, and just walked.

'We must be nearly home now, aren't we?' Lucy said.

Mum looked at the map. 'We're about a quarter of the way round,' she said.

Lucy opened her mouth to say something extremely cross, and Dad said quickly, 'I know. Let's play I Spy.' He looked over to a field with two ponies in it. 'I Spy with my little eye something beginning with P.'

'Pokehead!' Lucy shouted.

Dad laughed. 'No, not Pokehead.'

'Pokehead!' Will shouted.

'Don't be silly, Will, ' Dad said. 'Lucy just guessed that.'

'Look,' Mum said. 'There's Pokehead.'

Dad turned and looked. Standing at the end of a lane just ahead was Pokehead. It was such a shock to see her there at first he couldn't believe it. Then round the corner behind her came Tim, and behind him, their mum, Philippa.

Will and Lucy ran forwards to meet their friends, and they all started talking at once.

'What are you doing here, Peachey?'

'Walking. Mum made us.'

'Our mum made us too.'

'I hate walks. Nothing happens on walks.'

'Our dad got told off for trying steal part of somebody's garden. But nothing else happened.'

'I tried to hide, but Tim spoilt it by finding me.'

'You fell out of the tree on top of me. I don't call that finding.'

It turned out that the Peacheys were going on the same walk as the Quigleys. Everyone was pleased about this, especially Mum and Dad and Philippa.

'I'm afraid the children don't like walks much,' Philippa said. 'But I had to get them out of the house. Ben's gone off with Elizabeth for the day.'

Just then her mobile phone rang. 'Hello,' she said. 'Yes. Oh no. No, I can't, we're out walking. Wait a minute.' She turned to Mum and Dad. 'It's Ben. His train's broken down and he and Elizabeth are stranded. He wants me to fetch them in the car.'

'That's all right,' Mum said. 'You go back. We'll carry on with the children.'

'Are you sure?'

'Yes, of course. Now that they've got their friends, I'm sure they won't be any bother at all.'

Once Philippa had gone, Mum and Dad had a talk about the children. 'I'm worried about Pokehead,' Dad said. 'She's always answering back.'

'Don't worry. They'll all be chatting and playing. With a bit of luck, we might even be able to have a chat ourselves.'

They looked at the map together, and Dad called to the children. 'OK, everyone,' he said. 'This way.'

'I don't want to go that way,' Pokehead said.

'But this is the way,' Dad said.

'You go that way then,' Pokehead said. 'And we'll go this way.'

'Now, Pokehead. No arguing.'

'I'm not arguing.'

'And no answering back.'

'You're answering me back.'

Dad thought about this. 'Get the boiled sweets out,' he said to Mum.

For a while it was possible to bribe Pokehead to stay with them, but she hankered after other routes. Every time they came to a fork in the path, she wanted to go the other way. Dad said things like: 'You don't know where you'll end up if you go that way.' And Pokehead would say: 'It's a shortcut.' Or: 'Well, it's better than that way.' And sometimes Tim would say, for the sake of joining in: 'I hate walks.'

Will was very excited because of meeting Tim. He showed him an owl pellet that he'd found earlier, and they spent a long time examining it.

'Is it poo?' Tim said.

'It's sick.'

'It's sick all right, but is it poo?'

Lucy was also pleased to have met Pokehead. They talked about the best skipping songs, and Pokehead showed Lucy some beautiful bruises on her arm which she said you could get by sucking.

But neither Will nor Lucy were sure they wanted to run off with Pokehead on one of her shortcuts.

They came to

another fork in the path.

'This way,' Dad said.

Pokehead looked up and down. 'I think we should go this way.'

Dad said to Mum, 'Pass the sweets.'

'There aren't any left.'

Dad looked at Pokehead but before he could say anything, Lucy said, 'I know a game we can play, Dad. Let's all go your way, but you go first, and we'll track you.'

'Track me?'

'Yes. Like Red Indians. You don't have to leave arrows. We'll just find you.'

Pokehead smiled. 'I like that,' she said. 'We have to track you and not be seen, so we have to hide and disguise ourselves as bushes, and smear ourselves with . . .'

'Yes,' Lucy said. 'All that.'

'All right,' Dad said.

Mum and Dad started down the path. Will, Lucy, Pokehead and Tim crouched down in the goose grass and practised holding their breath for about five minutes. Eventually Will said, 'OK. Let's go.' And

they slithered forwards, Indian-style, through the grass.

It was good being Indian trackers. One by one they ran doubled-up across a mossy bank and dived full length behind an old tree stump. Will's was the best dive, but Tim injured himself the most. They crawled across a short grassy stretch and flopped into a ditch full of interesting rubbish like more owl pellets and shotgun cases. Every few minutes, Mum or Dad turned round to look for them, and, when they did, the children would hurl themselves onto the ground or bounce sideways into a hedge or run up a tree. Disguise was very important. Will stuffed grasses into his shirt. Tim put quite a bit of hedge down his back. Lucy plaited seven purple foxgloves into her hair. And Pokehead rubbed herself from top to toe with black mud from a bog.

Another thing they did was develop a special sign language, so they could communicate without making a noise.

A chopping hand meant 'Go back!' A thumbed-up nose meant 'The pigs have lost us.' Five fingers pressed to the ground meant 'Squash yourself, Dude.' And a wide-open mouth meant 'I've just sat on something odd.'

In this way they covered about half a mile.

Mum and Dad walked ahead peacefully, chatting.

'Are they still behind us?' Mum asked.

Dad looked back. 'Yes,' he said. 'Will's just jumped into a rhododendron and Lucy's pretending to be the Chelsea flower show. And the dark shadow by that wall is either Pokehead or a thing of unspeakable evil.'

'This is very nice,' Mum said. 'It's ages since we've had the chance to have a good chat without being interrupted.'

After a while, Mum and Dad came to a long, narrow lane between drystone walls.

The Indian trackers stopped.

'How are we going to track them down there?' Tim said.

'There's no cover,' Lucy said. 'They'll see us.'

Pokehead examined the trail. 'I know a shortcut,' she said. 'Follow me.'

Without thinking, they all followed. They jumped over a fence and went across a field of grass towards an old barn.

'We can circle round,' Pokehead said. 'And take them by surprise.'

They liked the sound of that. They scooted past the old barn and ran along a hedge until they came to a stream.

'This way,' Pokehead said.

Lucy looked at the stream. 'Are you sure?'

'What's the matter? Are you frightened?'

They got over the stream. Will caught a soaker, though no one noticed.

'Caught a soaker back there,' he said to everyone as they ran on. 'Not that I noticed.'

They went through a field of low, twisted vegetables they couldn't identify to a country road, and along the road for a bit, and over a stile into a field full of sheep.

They were walking by now.

Lucy said, 'This field is partly full of sheep and partly full of sheep poo.'

At the end of the field, they stopped for a breather.

'Well,' Tim said to Pokehead. 'Where are we?'

Pokehead shrugged. 'I expect we're lost. But who cares about being lost?'

The other three put their hands up.

Tim and Pokehead had an argument, and then a small fight.

'Wait,' Will said. 'We have to think how we can find Mum and Dad again. They can't be far away. We just have to decide which way to go.'

They all looked around them. One way there was a field of sheep, one way there was a wood, one way there was a road, and the other way there was a hill.

Lucy moved a bit closer to Will. 'I don't know which way it is,' she said in a quiet voice.

'Don't worry,' Will said. He put his hand up to his eyes to scan the countryside. It didn't help him see but it made him feel better. 'Look,' he said. 'See that church spire over there? That's the church by our cycle track. That's the way we have to go.'

'Are you sure, Will?'

'I think so.'

They all set off.

Mum and Dad walked peacefully down the lane, chatting.

'Are they still behind us?' Mum asked.

'I think so,' Dad said. 'They've got better at tracking, though. I haven't seen them for a while.'

'At least they're happy,' she said. 'And so are we. This is turning out to be a very good Mother's Day walk. Tell me again about that book you're reading.'

And they walked on happily, chatting.

Will, Lucy, Tim and Pokehead went across a field and came to a wood.

'Which way now?'

They stood there scratching their heads.

'I hate being lost,' Tim said.

'I like it,' Pokehead said.

Tim and Pokehead had another fight.

'I think we should go through the wood,' Will said. He climbed over the stile. On the other side of the stile was a sign. The sign said: *Beware. Adders.* He climbed back.

'No,' he said. 'I don't think that's the right way. I reckon we should cut across this field instead.'

At the end of the field was an electric fence.

'I like electric fences,' Pokehead said. 'Do you like them?'

Lucy shook her head. Pokehead got a stick and hit the

fence. With a loud cry she flew backwards and fell to the ground thrashing and twitching.

'Pokehead!' They all rushed over to her. 'Are you all right? Did you get a shock?'

Pokehead got to her feet. 'No, I was just practising. Shall I do it again?'

They went through a gate into another field just like the last one, and began to walk across it.

'Will, I don't like being lost.'

Will held Lucy's hand. 'Oh, we're not really lost,' he said. 'We're just sort of . . . loose.'

'Are we still going towards the church spire?'

Will looked all round to see if he could see it anywhere. 'Probably,' he said.

He went over to Tim and said quietly, 'I think we might need to come up with a plan soon.'

'This is all Pokehead's fault,' Tim said crossly.

'Yes, but we still need a plan.'

'You hold her and I'll hit her.'

'No, I mean a plan for finding Mum and Dad. I don't think we're just going to catch sight of them.'

As he said that, Lucy shouted, 'Look! Mum and Dad!'

'Where?'

'On the path over there. They've just gone behind that hedge.'

'Are you sure it was them?'

'I think so.'

They all began to run. As they ran, they shouted. Will and Lucy shouted, 'Mum!' and 'Dad!' Tim shouted, 'Wait!' And Pokehead shouted, 'Our way was much better than your way, I bet you haven't been blown up by an electric fence!'

They reached a broad, green path bordered by hawthorns, and dashed bellowing round a corner, where they found

two elderly strangers peering at them nervously.

The lady said, 'Are you all right? We heard a lot of wild noise. Is something chasing you?'

Will explained about looking for Mum and Dad.

'I think we may just have seen them,' the man said. 'What does your mum look like?'

Will thought about it. 'Well, she's quite funny-looking, really. She looks pretty friendly most of the time, but when she's cross she has this smile, and it's not really a smile, it's more of a warning.'

The man looked blankly at Will. 'What's she wearing?' he asked.

Will looked blankly back.

'Fawn trousers and a blue jumper,' Lucy said promptly. 'And she's pretty,' she added, with a look at Will.

'And is she with a man carrying a large rucksack?' the lady said.

They nodded.

'Yes, we passed them five minutes ago. You'll easily catch up with them. Just keep to the path.' The man pointed with his stick.

The children thanked him and dashed off.

'I hope they stick to the path,' the man said to his wife. 'I forgot to tell them not to cut across the field in case the farmer's put his bull in. But I don't think he has. I didn't see it anyway.'

Now that they had nearly caught up with Mum and Dad, the children were feeling much happier. They ran up the path until they reached the top of a small hill. Down below, on the other side of a field, they could see Mum and Dad walking along peacefully, deep in conversation.

Lucy gave a squeak of relief.

'Oh, well,' Pokehead said. 'It was good while it lasted.'

They set off down the path.

'Look at them talk,' Will said. 'They probably don't even realize we've been lost.'

'We can pretend we've been tracking them all the time,' Tim said.

They came to a gate.

'I know,' Pokehead said. 'We can take a short cut through this field without them seeing us, and give them a surprise.'

By this time, the others had grown wary of Pokehead's short cuts. But they weren't too worried because they could see Mum and Dad.

Will looked into the field. 'I suppose it's all right,' he said. 'It's just an empty field.'

They climbed over the gate, and set off in a low, crouching run across the grass. They could see Mum and Dad's heads moving above the hedge on the other side as they walked along, chatting.

'If they glance over here,' Will said, 'flatten

yourselves.' In fact they didn't glance, but the children flattened themselves several times, just to be on the safe side. Soon they were enjoying themselves as much as ever.

When they were about halfway across the field, Lucy said, 'Oh look. There's a cow.'

They looked.

'It's a biggish cow,' Will said.

'With horns,' Tim said.

Even Pokehead was impressed. They stood staring at the gigantic creature grazing in its grassy corner.

Lucy said, 'What if it's a bull?'

Tim said, 'They don't do much, bulls. Our uncle in Ireland used to have a bull. It didn't do much. Anyway, they only chase you if you're wearing something bright red.'

'That's right,' Will said. 'And who'd be stupid enough to go on a country walk wearing something bright red?'

They all looked at him. He looked down at his football jersey. 'Oh,' he said.

They all looked back at the bull.

'I think it's seen us,' Lucy said. 'Or, at least, it's seen you, Will.'

'Quick!' Tim said to Will. 'Take your jersey off.'

'What am I going to do with it?'

'Hide it!'

'Where am I going to hide it?'

'I don't know. Put it in your mouth or something.'

'Don't be stupid. It's a full replica shirt, I can't get it in my mouth.'

'Put it down your shorts then.'

Will stuffed it down his shorts. His shorts

became very thick, but nobody minded.

'It's coming this way,' Lucy said.

They all looked, one last time.

'Run!'

They went as fast as they could back the way they had come, towards the gate, shouting things like, 'Faster!' and 'Mind out!' and 'I can't run with thick shorts!'.

Behind them, they heard the lumbering thump of hooves.

Mum and Dad were walking along the lane talking about cookery books when they heard a noise like a stampede of cave men.

'Look,' Mum said. 'A bull charging across the field.'

'It's chasing some people,' Dad said. 'Some fools have gone into its field.'

They squinted across the field.

'Oh no!' they said together.

Will and Tim reached the gate in the far wall at more or less the same time and started to scramble over. Pokehead and

Lucy were coming up behind. The bull was still chasing them, and it was getting closer.

'Quick!' Will shouted to Pokehead and Lucy. 'Come on!'

Just then Lucy tripped and fell. Pokehead didn't realize at first and carried on running. Then she looked back and stopped.

'Oh no,' Will said.

Everything seemed to come to a halt. Will and Tim crouched motionless on top of the gate. Mum and Dad stared wide-eyed from behind the hedge at the far side. Pokehead stood fixed to the ground in the field. All of 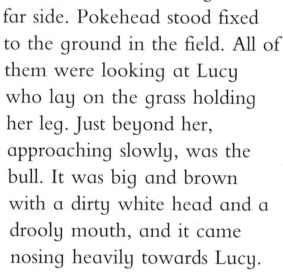 them were looking at Lucy who lay on the grass holding her leg. Just beyond her, approaching slowly, was the bull. It was big and brown with a dirty white head and a drooly mouth, and it came nosing heavily towards Lucy.

Before anyone could do anything, Pokehead turned

round and marched back towards it.

'Oh no,' Will said again.

Pokehead didn't stop or slow down, she marched straight up to Lucy, and stood facing the bull. The bull stopped a few feet away and glared at her. Pokehead glared back. There was silence for a moment.

The bull shook his head and made a slappy, snorty noise with his loose mouth.

Pokehead shook her head back at him and blew an enormous raspberry.

That surprised the bull. It backed away, turning its head from side to side, as if suddenly lost. Ignoring it, Pokehead helped Lucy up, and they went slowly together towards the gate. The bull stayed where it was, looking nervous.

As Will and Tim were helping the girls over the gate, there were footsteps down the path, and Mum and Dad came running round the corner of the hedge. Mum hugged Lucy, and Dad started patting them all on the head, and for a long time no one knew quite what to say, and in fact it seemed important not to say anything at all.

Only when they finally went on with their walk did they talk about it properly. Lucy explained how a molehill had tripped her up, and Will demonstrated how difficult it is to run with thick shorts, and Tim told everyone again how it was all the fault of Pokehead's short cuts.

Mum and Dad kept asking everyone questions. Most of all they asked Pokehead about facing up to the bull, which they thought was one of the bravest things they'd ever seen.

Pokehead herself seemed very unimpressed by what she'd done.

'Didn't you feel scared when it stared at you?'

'No one can outstare me. I'm the best in the school for staring.'

'She is,' Tim said. 'She's got horrible eyes.'

'But what about when it snorted at you?'

Pokehead shrugged. 'I just answered it back.'

'She's always getting told off for answering back,' Tim said.

'I'm beginning to feel quite sorry for the bull,' Dad said quietly to Mum.

They walked homewards along the path, but in five minutes the spell of excitement wore off, and the children remembered gloomily that they were still on a walk.

'How far have we got to go?' Will asked.

'We've been walking all day,' Lucy complained.

'I hate walks,' Tim said. 'They're so boring.'

In with Dad

In With Dad

The Quigleys lived in quite a small house. That wasn't so bad. You can do things in small houses you can't do in big ones. In the Quigley's house, if you aimed right you could throw a paper aeroplane all the way from the back room and hit someone talking on the telephone at the front of the hall. You could jump from halfway up the stairs and land next to the front door without hurting yourself, and doing hardly any damage to the floorboards. Best of all, you could make yourself heard anywhere in the house without having to get off the toilet.

Mum and Dad didn't always see it like that. Dad sometimes said he thought the house was too small. One day, he asked the children if they would like to move to a bigger house.

'Don't you like this house?' Lucy asked.

'Well, Poodle. I think we may need more space.'

'Why?'

'Well. You're bigger. And bouncier. And you're much more everywhere-all-the-time than you used to be. The thing about small houses is that you have to be well-behaved in them, so as not to deafen people or break their legs.'

'What sort of bigger house do you mean?' Will asked. Will was always interested in practical details.

Mum said one with more bedrooms and a bigger garden.

'Will there be a treehouse in it?'

'I don't know. Perhaps. But you and Lucy could have your own rooms.'

'Will we have televisions in them?'

'Well, we'll see.'

'Will we be able to do martial arts in the back room?'

'Will, we're talking about buying a new house, not a sports and leisure complex.'

Will and Lucy said they'd think about it. They lay awake in bed that night, thinking about it.

'They said we could have our own rooms. Do you want a room of your own?'

'I don't know. Do you?'

'I don't know either.'

They lay there not knowing.

Eventually, Will said, 'If you had your own room you could have lots of pink things in it. The sorts of things I don't allow. That would be nice for you.'

Lucy agreed. 'And you could have your music player next to your bed.'

Will sat up. 'And my electric guitar.'

Lucy said, 'But you haven't got an electric guitar.'

'No, but I could get one for my new room. If you have a new house, it stands to reason you've got to get new things to put in it. Otherwise, what are you going to do with all that space?' He lay back. 'An electric guitar in one of those travelling cases. And my own computer on a desk under the window. And security cameras above the door so I'd know who's coming and if they're friendly.'

That sounded better. He lay back, and Lucy heard him give a sigh, and soon they both fell asleep thinking about new things to put in their new rooms in their new bigger house.

Over the next few days the children were very excitable, thinking about their new house and all the new things to put in it.

Mum, however, didn't seem so excited. She kept saying things like 'I'll be sad to leave this house,' and 'I hope we'll be able to find somewhere else as nice.' Even Dad seemed a bit sad, now that he'd suggested moving.

'Don't you want to move to a bigger house?' Lucy asked Mum.

She shook her head. 'Not really. But Dad's probably right. We do need more space.'

Lucy was very sympathetic. 'Never mind, Mum. Just think of all your new things.'

Mum looked puzzled. 'What new things?'

'For your room.'

Mum was still puzzled. Lucy felt very sorry for her. She gave her a hug and said, 'I know what. Why don't you make a list of all the nice new things you'll get? That'll cheer you up. Will and I have made our lists already.'

Mum started to tell Lucy, quite firmly, that moving house was not all about buying new things, but at that moment Will came into the back room, being excitable. He was so excitable he forgot about the back room being too short for cartwheels.

'Not in the house!' Mum said.

Lucy did a cartwheel too. She was better at cartwheels than Will, so it was only fair.

'Not in the house!' Mum said, more loudly.

'Just watch my best cartwheel,' Lucy said.

But Will didn't want to be outdone. 'Watch my worst cartwheel!' he said. 'Mum, you're not watching.'

'Will, no!'

He whirled sideways with a yell, crashed against the clothes hanger, skidded across the floor, trailing damp sweaters and underwear, and spat out a sock. 'Oops,' he said. 'It wasn't meant to be quite so bad.'

Mum was cross. 'Think of what Dad said about being well-behaved in small houses,' she said. 'Think of the Family Rules.'

She pointed to the Family Rules, which were pinned up on the toy cupboard door. They all looked. Someone had been writing on them again. Underneath the third family rule *(Think Before You Speak),* someone had  written *No Farting.* And underneath that: *No Noughty Stuf.* And underneath that, in grown-up writing: *For God's Sake Put the Car Keys Back in the Drawer.* Mum decided not to discuss the Family Rules.

After they had been sent outside, Lucy and Will went to see Timothy, Elizabeth and Pokehead, their best friends, who lived just up the street. The Peacheys lived in a house just like the Quigleys', but two doors away, with another house in between. The other house was owned by someone called the Dingbat. They sat in the Peacheys' garden, drinking squash and chatting.

'Guess what?' Will said. 'We're going to move to a bigger house.' He grinned. 'With new things for our rooms.'

Lucy grinned too. 'And a new back room big enough for cartwheels.'

They both grinned. But Elizabeth, Timothy and Pokehead didn't grin.

'Where are you moving to?' Elizabeth asked.

'We don't know. Why?'

'Well, if you move away, we won't be able to see you so much.'

Will and Lucy stopped grinning. Suddenly they realized what moving house would mean. Before, they had been so excited about treehouses and new things, they'd forgotten all about the moving bit of moving house.

'Even if you don't move very far away,' Elizabeth said, 'we won't be able to pop into each other's houses.'

'We won't be able to have weed-throwing games between our gardens, like we do now,' Pokehead said.

'And we won't be able to climb out of our garden and crawl along the Dingbat's shed roof into your garden, and get shouted at by the Dingbat,' Tim said.

Lucy was upset. 'I've changed my mind,' she said. 'I don't want to move to a new bigger house any more. I want to stay here, in our street.'

Will held her hand, even though there were other people watching. He was sad too. 'I got carried away thinking of new things,' he said sadly. It was true. The last few days he'd been thinking only about the new house. Now he thought about the old house. It might be small, but it was nice. He remembered how much he liked it. He liked the rose bushes in the front garden, even though they smelled of cat, and he liked the

back room, even though it wasn't quite big
enough for cartwheels. He even liked
sharing a room with Lucy. Best of all, he
liked living close to Elizabeth, Timothy and
Pokehead.

'I don't want to move either,' he said.
'But the problem is,' he said, sighing, 'Mum
and Dad do.'

'That's OK,' Pokehead said. 'You just
have to stop them. My mum and dad are
always wanting to do things, and I stop
them.'

'Usually I help stop them,' Tim said.

'But the advert's gone in the paper already,' Will said. 'And Dad's going to put up the *For Sale* sign, and people will be coming to look round. It's too late.'

'There are always things you can do to stop mums and dads,' Pokehead said briskly. 'Even when it's late.'

Lucy dried her face with her sleeve. 'Like what?' she asked.

They began to talk about it.

Will and Lucy were still talking about it that evening, after Mum and Dad had said goodnight and turned the light out.

'I really like this house,' Will said from the top bunk. 'I've lived here all my life, and I don't see why we should move just because Mum and Dad want us to. They haven't lived here all their lives. You'd think they'd understand that.'

'I really like our house too, Will,' Lucy said. 'I like the kitchen, and the stairs, and I like that skirty board thing by the door I stand on to reach the door handle. And I like our room. Do you like our room, Will?'

Will nodded in the dark. 'And what about the curtains in the back room downstairs? They're brilliant curtains, I bet you can't get curtains like that in other houses. Do you remember when we hid behind them when you were really small, and Dad couldn't find us for ages, and when he did, I'd missed my clarinet lesson?'

Lucy grinned in the dark. 'And the bath,' she said. 'I love our bath. It's just the right size, and it feels so friendly, and when the hot water tap gets stuck I can always shout for you to come and turn it off.'

'Unless the door handle's fallen off again, and then I can't get in,' Will said happily. 'I love our bath too. I don't want to ever have a bath in another bath.'

'Neither do I. But what are we going to do then?'

There was a silence.

'I don't know,' Will said. 'I don't think Timothy and Pokehead's ideas were very good.'

'*I* don't,' Lucy said. 'I don't want to run away, and I don't want to start a fire in the toilet, even if it is only a small one just to scare people off.'

'No,' Will said. 'And I don't want to live in Tim's cellar for six months until they give in to our ransom demands.'

'So what are we going to do?' Lucy said after a pause.

Will sighed. 'I don't know. I have to go to sleep now.'

'Will you know tomorrow?'

'I don't know yet. Go to sleep, and I'll tell you in the morning.'

But in the morning, Will still didn't know. And it turned out to be a terrible morning.

At breakfast, Dad showed them the advert for their house in the newspaper. The advert said things like *tasteful modern rear extension,* and there was a colour photograph of the front of the house all lit up in the sun looking friendly. It didn't say anything about not-enough-room-for-cartwheels, or door handles that fell off.

Will and Lucy sat scowling at the newspaper.

'What's the matter?' Dad said. 'Don't you think people will want to buy it?'

'That's just it,' Will said. 'I think people *will* want to buy it.'

'We've decided we don't want people to buy it,' Lucy said. 'Not the tasting modern rear thing, not any of it.'

Dad smiled sympathetically. He could be very sympathetic when he wanted to. 'I know how you feel,' he said. 'It's a nice house, isn't it? We'll miss it. But you'll feel differently when we're in a new place, I promise.' He replaced his sympathetic look with the determined look that made him look cross-eyed.

But after breakfast the morning got worse. Mum said that the house needed tidying before people came to look round. She said that from now on it had to be kept tidy *all the time,* even Will and Lucy's room, which, as Will pointed out, wasn't meant to be tidy.

After a week of cleaning the house, everyone was feeling either sad or angry, even Mum and Dad. Mum took to sighing and saying gloomy things like, 'I'll miss the garden when we're gone.' Dad took to snarling and saying things like, 'They have to do this sort of thing in prison, you know.'

Having to clean all the time changed Dad's mind about moving house. 'I know I said we should,' he said to Mum, as he cleaned the cooker. 'But now I'm not really sure.' He sniffed. Having to clean all the time was so awful, he was coming down with a cold.

'Me neither,' Mum said. 'But we have to think of the children.'

Upstairs, where Will and Lucy were tidying their room for the third time, Will was saying bitterly, 'Do you know what gets me? They don't even consider us. All they think about is themselves.'

At last they finished the cleaning. The house was brighter and smarter and oddly unfamiliar.

'I had no idea the kitchen walls were white,' Mum said.

'I had no idea we had so much space in our room, Will,' Lucy said.

'I've no idea where my *Beanos* are,' Will said gloomily. 'You didn't have to hunt for them before; if you wanted one it was always just there.'

By the time the first people were coming to look round the house, Dad's cold was much worse. 'You'll have to show them round,' he said to Mum. But Mum reminded him that she was going on a course.

Dad was in despair. 'But I ought to be in bed, not showing people round.'

'The children will help,' Mum said. 'Just make sure they're well-behaved.'

Dad looked towards the Family Rules.

Someone had been writing on them again. The words *No Swaring* were clearly visible at the bottom in thick blue felt-tip.

Dad opened his mouth, saw Mum looking at him, and shut it again. Lucy and Will were bickering in their room. Dad shouted up to them to stop. Then Mum went out. The last thing she heard was Dad shouting up the stairs, 'I'm ill! How can I be Polite and Pleasant when I'm ill?'

Dad, Will and Lucy had a meeting.

'This is a meeting about showing people round the house,' Dad said. He coughed into his handkerchief. 'It's a meeting about being Polite and Pleasant, and being Helpful and Honest, and smiling and looking people in the eye when they say hello to you.'

He sneezed and sat down heavily at the kitchen table, and put his head in his hands.

'You look terrible, Dad,' Will said.

Dad groaned.

'You really do, Dad,' Lucy said. 'It's hard to say how bad you look. Do you remember that dead fish we saw on holiday?'

Dad propped himself up on one elbow. 'I think I'll have to go to bed for a little nap before people get here,' he said. 'When I get up we'll talk about showing them round, and the sorts of questions they might ask, and what to say to them.'

'OK,' Lucy said. 'Have a nice rest.'

He went upstairs, and they heard him close the bedroom door, and then the house was quiet.

'Poor Dad,' Lucy said. 'He needs a good sleep.'

'It's odd, isn't it?' Will said. 'The way he looked just like that fish.'

'What shall we do now, Will?'

Will thought. 'We could go and ask Elizabeth and Timothy and Pokehead if they want to come round to play, just for a while. They'd enjoy a nice clean house like this.'

'That's a good idea,' Lucy said brightly. But before they could move, there was a knock on the door.

'Perhaps that's them now,' Will said. 'I'll go.'

'No, I will!' Lucy shouted.

One of the good things about a small house is that you can get to the front door really quickly from just about anywhere. They raced there and struggled hard with each other to open it. First Lucy got it part way open. Then Will slammed it shut. Then Will yanked it open again, and for a while they both pulled and pushed, and it jerked open and shut, open and shut, until finally with a great heave, Will forced it back all the way, and stood panting and grinning savagely in the open doorway. But it wasn't Elizabeth, Timothy and Pokehead he saw in front of him. It was a strange man and lady. The man had brown hair and glasses,

and the lady was wearing a red knitted sweater.

For a moment they all looked at each other, then Lucy said, 'Oh. Have you come to look at our house?'

'Don't be silly, Lucy,' Will said. 'They're not due till after lunch.'

'Yes, we have actually,' said the man. 'The estate agent said any time was fine.'

Will's face fell. 'Oh,' he said.

Lucy took over. 'Please come in,' she said politely, and they all went inside. 'Be Polite and Pleasant,' she hissed at Will as she passed him.

When they were standing in the front room, the lady asked if their parents were in, and Will and Lucy explained about Mum being out and Dad being in bed. 'He's ill,' Will said. 'And you really wouldn't want to see him looking the way he does.'

'Like a fish,' Lucy put in.

'If you've ever seen a dead fish,' Will said. 'Anyway, he asked us to start showing

you round and answering your questions. If you've got any,' he added politely. 'You don't have to have questions if you don't want.'

'This is a very nice house,' the lady said. 'You've been very lucky living here.'

Will nodded glumly, and they went out of the front room down the hall.

'Will,' Lucy hissed. 'You have to tell them things.'

'What sort of things?' Will hissed back.

'You know. Tell them what everything is.'

When they got into the back room, Will said, 'This is the kitchen, and that's the bit built on at the end. Down there.'

'The tasting modern rear thing,' Lucy said helpfully.

'Yes, that's it,' Will said. 'Down there, past the Welsh dresser. That's the Welsh dresser, with the broken door. Lucy broke it.'

'I didn't,' Lucy said. 'You pushed me.'

'She sort of fell,' Will said. 'And broke it. Anyway, Dad's going to fix it. Though he says that about lots of things in the house and never gets round to it.'

They came out of the back room, and went down the hall again.

'This is the hall again,' Will said, 'and these are the stairs, and those are the bannisters going up the stairs.'

As they went up the stairs, the bells of the church at the back of the house began to ring.

'What's that?' the woman asked.

Will put his head on one side and listened. 'I think it's the boiler,' he said at last. 'You can't hear properly because of those stupid bells. But the boiler's always

making this groaning noise. Which is OK,'
he added, 'as long as you turn the hot
water off as soon as you hear it. Otherwise,
Dad says it'll blow up.'

The woman looked funny. 'I meant the
bells actually,' she said. 'I like the sound of
bells.'

'You might not like them at six in the
morning on Sunday,' Will said. 'But at least
it gets us out of bed, Mum says.'

At the top of the stairs, Will looked

round. 'This is the bathroom,' he said. 'Careful the door handle doesn't fall off onto your foot. And here are some more stairs.'

'These are the stairs where I fell when I was small,' Lucy added proudly. 'And I bashed my face and it bled.'

'That's right,' Will said. 'If you look, you can still see the teethmarks in the wall.'

They showed the man and lady the spare bedroom, the study and their own room, and, for quite a long time, a new table football game, which they'd just been given.

Lucy and Will beat the man and lady 8–3. It was a bit chilly because the radiators had gone off, though Will helpfully demonstrated how Dad got them working again by bashing them at the exact right spot with the heel of his shoe.

'He always shouts when he does it,' he said. 'You don't have to shout though, if you don't want to,' he added politely.

The man asked if they could go out into the garden now, and they all went back downstairs, through the back room and out onto the patio.

'It's a good job you've come in the spring,' Will said, 'because it floods in the winter.'

'And what's up here?' the lady asked.

'Oh, that's just the side passage. You don't want to go up there. The drain's always getting blocked and it doesn't

smell too good. That's why we keep the kitchen window closed.'

The man and lady decided they didn't need to look round anymore.

'What about your questions?' Will asked. 'If you've got any.'

The man and lady said they didn't have any questions, the children had told them everything they needed to know.

After the man and lady had gone, Lucy said, 'You were good at telling them things, Will.'

Will was frowning. 'It's funny, though,' he said. 'They didn't seem so keen at the end.'

They both thought about this for a while.

'I don't think they liked the bit when you said the garden flooded,' Lucy said at last. 'Or when you explained about the lights going out all the time, and having to crawl into the cupboard under the stairs to turn them on again.'

'You're right,' Will said. 'Do you know what I think? I think I put them off. By accident, I mean.' He sighed. 'I don't suppose they'll want to buy our house any more.'

They sat in silence.

'What happens,' Lucy asked after a while, 'if you put everyone off? Does that mean that no one will want to buy our house?'

Will stared at her. A strange look came over his face. It was sort of surprised and cunning, and it made him look slightly mad. 'If I put everyone off,' he said slowly, 'then . . . we won't have to move any more.'

The same surprised, cunning, slightly-mad look came over Lucy's face.

'It's not lying,' Will said quickly. 'It's

being Polite and Pleasant, and Helpful and Smiling at People in the Eyes, and everything else that the Family Rules say. It's just that it accidentally puts them off.'

Will and Lucy were so pleased, they got up and danced round their nice old front room. Then there was another knock on the door.

'Here's another lot want showing round,' Will said. 'Come on.'

He opened the door and smiled at the man and lady standing there. 'Please come in,' he said. 'But be careful with the door, if you don't close it right it can fall off and hit you on the head.'

A week later, Mum, Dad, Will and Lucy had a meeting about moving house.

'We've got some disappointing news,' Mum said. 'It's not proving very easy to sell

our house. After all those people who came to see it last Saturday, no one has offered to buy it.'

Will and Lucy didn't say anything.

'It's a real mystery,' Dad said. 'A nice house like this.'

Mum sighed. 'The estate agent wants us to lower the price. But we can't.'

Will and Lucy still didn't say anything. Their faces were expressionless.

Dad said, 'In any case, Mum and I have been thinking again, and we're not sure we want to sell our house after all. It's a nice house, really. I know it might be a disappointment to you, after all the talk of rooms of your own, and treehouses and things.'

Will said, 'Ah, well.' He used a flat tone of voice.

Lucy said, 'Oh, well.' She used the same tone of voice.

Mum and Dad looked at them, and Will and Lucy looked at the wall.

'So you're not too disappointed?' Dad asked.

Will and Lucy looked at each other. 'Well,' Lucy said. 'The thing is . . .'

'Yes?' Mum said.

'Lucy's right,' Will said. 'It's just that . . .'

Mum and Dad looked at them. 'What?' they said.

Will took a deep breath and said, 'Well, don't get any ideas about good behaviour all the time, but the thing is: we love our house.'

'Not just the house, Will,' Lucy said.

'No,' he said. 'The curtains as well.'

'And the stairs where I fell and bit the wall,' Lucy said.

'Don't make us move,' Will said. 'We don't want to move.'

'We don't,' Lucy said. 'We want to stay here and not have baths anywhere else.'

After it was finally clear that no one wanted to move, and Dad had thanked Will and Lucy for making him finally realize it, they made hot chocolate and talked quite a bit about their house. They all walked round it, admiring how very clean and new-looking it was, and talking about the places where Will liked to cartwheel into the wet washing, and where Lucy had bit the wall, and where Dad always stood so as to shout loudest up the stairs, and where Mum skipped surprisingly well to old skipping songs.

And afterwards, Will and Lucy went to call for Elizabeth, Timothy and Pokehead, just up the street.